About the Author

Quinton Perry is an educator, poet, writer, and author of the new poetry collection *Blues on The Ceiling Fan.* Influenced by his nomadic experiences of growing up in the inner city of Baltimore, global travels, and life living abroad, his writing offers a unique perspective on the world at large. He writes to inspire.

Blues on the Ceiling Fan

Quinton Perry

Blues on the Ceiling Fan

Olympia Publishers
London

www.olympiapublishers.com
OLYMPIA PAPERBACK EDITION

A CIP catalogue record for this title is
available from the British Library.

ISBN: 978-1-78830-875-5

First Published in 2021

Olympia Publishers
Tallis House
2 Tallis Street
London
EC4Y 0AB
Printed in Great Britain

Dedication

For the orphans, foster children, downtrodden, displaced, and those that find themselves in a dark place.

For the social workers, teachers, mentors, and volunteers that find inspiration in the words as they appear.

Acknowledgements

I would like to sincerely thank the wonderful team at Olympia Publishers and all those who had a hand in bringing life to my vison of *Blues on The Ceiling Fan* for readership.

A calm heart and steady hands paint cautiously as you tend to your land, for you are the designer.

Such Is Life

I am poor and you are rich,

I am hungry and I am sick.

Little by little I fade away,

"Such is life," you always say.

Who am I?

Nothing —

The world we live in is full of haves and the have not,

It is not your fault that I didn't get a spot.

"Such is life," you always say.

This is a game you will always play,

For I am rich, and you are poor.

A Cold Birth

Cold was the wind abreast my face,

as empty stares of nature filled the place.

Encompassed by anger, frustration, and hate,

my mere existence solidified my fate.

To quell the cries of the broken peace,

I was gifted a dumpster as my place to sleep.

Food Chain

You stand there interlocked with me at night,

you look at me with fear during the day.

I am your prey yet also the predator,

I am the night and you are the day.

You hate me yet you love me,

you need me yet you don't want me.

I am the night and you are the prey,

I am the predator and you are the day.

You are me; I am you…

Human.

Imagination Escape

He dreamed because he had no other choice,

he had only known hopelessness,

he had only seen death.

A Bomb in the Market Place

As the sun shines and faces fill places, empty souls walk.

The cascade of emptiness blanketed upon still bodies —
void of life.

The screaming crows inviting relatives for lunch to inspect
the scene.
As the sun shines and faces fill places, empty souls walk.
The aroma sweet and sour singes the air, as lifeless hearts
lay scattered.
The unfixed light display in the busily market of colours
exists as normalcy.

As the sun shines and faces fill places, empty souls walk.

The impassive flood of despair flowing down the faces of
innocence.

Homeless — is one's heart confused by such darkness and
unconsciousness.

As the sunsets, faces fill graves; humanity walks.

Politics

You sleep on a bed,
They sleep on the ground.
You eat five meals a day,
They hope to eat one.
You
have access to clean water…
They
have none.
What have you done?

Hunger Pains

The dumpster is full,

my stomach is empty,

the fields reap so plenty.

I must go hungry,

because I do not have a penny,

as the dumpster remains full,

and my stomach remains empty.

P.T.S.D

Pain on the grip —

void is the barrel as it gazes at a blank face.

Tired is the bullet —

cold is the clip as it leaves stains on an empty place.

Screams of the heart —

tears in the dark as they drip down without a trace.

Desperate are the cries —

tight becomes the rope with fear of losing the race.

A Piece of Chocolate

What does it cost?
As I toil in the sun,
Steadily picking the cocoa beans under the eyes of a gun,
Tears of blood upon my fingertips begin to run,
While taste buds dance the chocolate swing on the tip of
your tongue.

Forgotten

If I died today —

no one would know,

I would melt away —

just like the snow.

Introvert

They all seemed to love me, but I hated them anyway.

I hated the way they looked;

Not their physical characteristics but how they looked at me.

Depressed Heart

The tranquil heart sees not what it gathers,

as all around causes it to shatter.

Mirth and meekness no longer a factor,

as the world decomposes of lifeless

matter.

Anomaly

I am clean as a bird bathing in a muddy puddle,

I am the perfect brick buried amongst the rubble,

I am the smile that emerges during the struggle,

I am the mute that hears clearly among the muddles,

I am…

Destiny Imagined

As the sunsets and the swells bellow against the cascading rocks,

The sudden rumble invades as a knock.

The sky falls flat and blankets the sea,

as perils of my sombre heart

squawk desperately.

A long time coming to be set free,

I watched as I soared away so graciously.

A Broken Vase

It took a piece of glass to see my reflection.

The secret is,

I was going to use it as a weapon.

Tears of Death

The faintest heart makes the loudest sound

as time begins to slip away.

The silent cry has the most tears

as pain begins to drip away.

Bike Lane

Peddling hastily,
the boisterous sounds of the city
conducting an enchanting orchestral melody in my ears.
My eyes were focused straight,
before I could hit the brakes.
I died by accident.

Ward of the State

I aged out of foster care and I survived.

Cemented in disguise as I navigate the lonely streets with insurmountable pride.

Pretending to understand the lies as I meticulously suffocate any family ties.

I aged out of foster care and I survived.

Tortured seldom at night by the anger and the hurt that disrupt my thoughts.

Days, become months, become years…

as I no longer forfeit tears for my kin absent years.

I aged out of foster care and I survived.

I walked away from the system with my head held high.

Blind Fate

As the vibrations of life tingle the spine,

Long walks through life inevitably blind,

Reminiscing about the things unable to define,

Searching only for —

A peace of mind,

A piece of mine.

Cry Your Last Tear

There was a little boy who had no home,

He was left all alone in the world to roam.

He cried all day and cried all night.

He cried until he gathered the courage to fight.

Lost at Sea

I can't help but wonder at your ever-flowing feet,
The crashing sounds against the rocks I hear.
Thrusting between my toes the chill of defeat,
As my path remains unclear.

Eyes of War

Fireworks lit up the sky in front of their eyes.

Screams of horror filled the air as their thighs caught fire.

Day — After — Day,

No parks or playgrounds to play,

An underground shelter is where they lay.

Hunger and thirst forever the plight,

Displaced in the middle of a heartless fight.

Awaiting assistance —

As days become harsher nights.

Wild Horse

Strong and swift running free,

stopping to see what is in front.

Wild at sight but calm as the rolling sea,

watching as the moon hunts.

Circle of Life

Earth between my toes,
planted in the grass of serendipity,
driven by time…
woven by those politically.
Manifested in fate,
the food chain rest upon my face,
defining the circle of life
as earth remains my resting place.

The Ant That Got Away

Strong I am,

but weak to the colony,

fearless but misguided by my hatred.

Calm as the patient sun,

but misleading as the wind that blows on a sunny day,

I was The Ant That Got Away.

Petals on the Ground

Patient and angelic fluttering gracefully through the air,
dancing as the wind played heavenly upon your stem.
Your petals translucent emitting radiantly under the
moonlight, immobilised in awe at the sight bestowed upon
your death.
To the ground you fell,
invisible to the world
landing in the garden of melancholy,
derived from the rooted mausoleum that yielded your life.
There you rested gracefully at peace.

Child Locked

You forgot me and I would forever wonder how,

I've seen your smile and you've seen mine too,

I heard you whisper that I was a dream come true.

I forgive you, intentional or not.

The car was hot.

I cried…

Left at the Orphanage

I never wanted you to go but you left anyway,

There was nothing I could do to make you stay,

My mouth unable to form any words away,

A babble and a gargle are all I could relay.

Unwanted by the Willow Tree

Paralysed, bounded by the growing roots smothering your existence.
Captivated by the unwanted attention, flinching only when the wind attempts to undress fate.
Grounded in the soil of infertility, happily waiting your turn remiss of time as you age and remain unclaimed.
The waning sun in a forest of billowy pillows masking the

chance to be set free,

as you wallow in shame —

to be unwanted by the Willow Tree.

Hidden Scars

Scars go unnoticed,
Hidden,
Underneath bandages of
Lies.

Sign Language

Unable to speak but I stare anyway.

Words unable to escape my mouth,

Having to use my hands as clay.

There I sit as you stand,

watching as your heart is approached in demand.

Our eyes connected at the moment we met,

Sweat fills my palms as fear holds me back.

Oh, how I wish I could ask you your name,

but I could never endure… the inevitable shame,

Until you

Signed Your Name.

Forget Me Not

Sounds of the clashing cans alerted me you were here,
your smiling eyes dim,
however, remain sincere.

Every day I meet you in our favourite place,
our initials carved in roots,
where I first gave chase.

You wander aimlessly as I watch in despair,
the fragrance of cinnamon hugs my nose,
kissing my hair.

Your fading memory knows no bounds,
losing sight of all things,
except this mound.

Upon my knee I extend the key,
the beginning of our life,
we vowed until the end it would be.

On this teeming day while in the park,
a glimmer of hope waltzed upon my heart.

You stopped,
there you shined directly in front of me,
Remembering the precious stone,
And where it longed to be.

Complicated Rehab

Easier to make excuses rather than to except what is true,

as we reminisce about the past and the things we did not do.

At the bottom of the abyss sitting contemplating life,

all the wrongs done that should be made right.

Selfishness is the underlying factor,

in attempts to understand the things that matter.

Pages in the book are filled in solitude,

looking at your own reflection not recognising you.

It is complicated the second time around, but things are looking up,

since you are already down.

Empty City

All I ever knew was guns and dope,

Where I am from that is the only hope.

Walking through the streets surrounded by trash,

Reminded every day as I sit in my class.

I know my teacher well —

I once caught him buying dope in the hood stairwell.

"Ignorant of alternatives," he said in class that day,

Scratching his arm where the track marks came to play.

The feeling of despair as I sit on the stoop,

Realising deep inside that dreams do not come true.

Institutionalised

To hear and not be seen —
What would life mean?
Try being Black
In a White man's dream...

The Eyes Behind the Lens

I saw your weeping eyes, as the vision of lies no longer disguised.
I witnessed the rage distributed among the film, as flashes of the camera enslaved us.
Images captured of smiles on faces from many different places.

Hearts shattered… Homes battered…

As captions no longer matter.

Elegant yet unbecoming of time, the mass incarceration of our minds,

unmoved by what we cannot define.

Holding this camera is beginning to feel like a

Crime.

Controlled Progression

Pain engulfs my eyes from the things I have seen.

The images constantly reflected in the cortex of my brain.

The smoke fills my lungs as the coal leaves a stain.

The little engine that could,

I think I can…

Addiction

A secret society some are a part of,
Initiation process is filled with the darkest
Love.
Hate is the pre-context to join the club
Filled with alcohol, money, sex, and lots of drugs.

Black on Black Crime

I am not afraid of Black,
I shouldn't have to be —
A walk along my block and Black is all you see.

Black face, Black mask, Black casings litter the street,
Black is one's heart as death surrounds me.

Stray was the bullet that hit my head —

I am not afraid of Black,
I shouldn't have to be —
But as I lay upon my back, Black is all I see.

Dead Leaves

A leaf is a leaf,

until it falls from the tree — Disconnected

for eternity.

Verbal Abuse

If the walls could talk what would they say?

The hell with you I am going away!

A sombre voice utters,

"Please stay."

Runaway

I am not going home today —
as the sun kissed my cheek,
my thumb guided the way.

Happy Demise

Death came with a smile
I laughed away,
buried in a grave —
the sounds
danced away.

Nightmares

The silence of darkness in the perilous fight,

As we seek to understand the purpose of life.

Moral consciousness manoeuvres the cortex right,

As time heal wounds, from cuts of the knife.

The solitude of one's thoughts eats away at the peace,

The white lies told haunting as we sleep.

Lost and Found

There will always exist a sense of longing in a life that was

born empty,

For the void cannot be filled with something that was

never there,

I always wondered what it would be like to have been
loved unconditionally —

I will always wonder.

The Shadow of Myself

Among the walls of uncertainty, I cannot sleep,

I toss and turn as my dreams begin to creep.

My eyes are restless as my heart is slow to beat,

Among the walls of uncertainty, I cannot sleep.

CPSIA information can be obtained
at www.ICGtesting.com
Printed in the USA
BVHW081201210321
603030BV00007B/1451